To my niece Charlotte, who came in the fall—L. T.
To my dear *Baba* for being an inspiration and a role
model to me—B. E.

SIMON & SCHUSTER BOOKS FOR YOUNG READERS
An imprint of Simon & Schuster Children's Publishing Division
1230 Avenue of the Americas, New York, New York 10020
Text copyright © 2006 by Lauren Thompson
Illustrations copyright © 2006 by Buket Erdogan
SIMON & SCHUSTER BOOKS FOR YOUNG READERS is a trademark
of Simon & Schuster, Inc.
Book design by Einav Aviram
Manufactured in China   0914 SCP
10 9 8 7
CIP data for this book is available from the Library of Congress.
ISBN-13: 978-0-689-85837-6
ISBN-10: 0-689-85837-X

MOUSE'S FIRST FALL

Lauren Thompson

ILLUSTRATED BY Buket Erdogan

SIMON & SCHUSTER BOOKS FOR YOUNG READERS
NEW YORK LONDON TORONTO SYDNEY

One cool fall day . . .

Mouse and Minka
came out to play!

Tumbling and twirling,
fall leaves fell all around.
"Look at all the colors!" said Minka.

Mouse saw
red leaves and yellow leaves
and orange leaves and brown leaves.

Pretty!

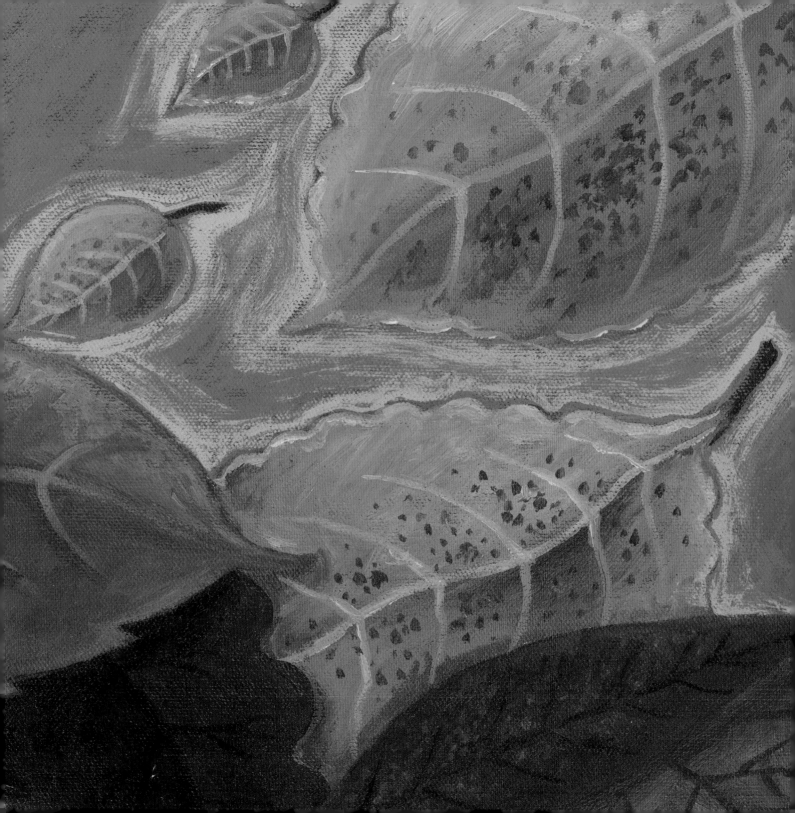

"Look at all the shapes!"
said Minka.

Mouse saw round leaves
and skinny leaves
and pointy leaves
and smooth leaves.

Yay!

"Let's run through the leaves!"
said Minka.

Mouse ran and skipped and kicked and swished through all the leaves.

Fun!

"Let's pile them up!"
said Minka.

Mouse piled the leaves high—
one leaf,
two leaves,
three leaves,
lots of leaves!

Yippee!

"What a big pile," said Minka.
"Let's jump in!"

Mouse leaped and jumped and plopped and rolled into the leaves.

Whee!

"I'm hiding," called Minka.
"Can you find me?"

Mouse peeked and poked
and peered between
the leaves.
Where could Minka be?

Then out popped Minka!
"Here I am!"

Hooray for Minka!
Hooray for Mouse!
Hip-hip-hooray for fall!